D1385439

HarperCollins *Children's Books*

First published in the USA by Philomel Books, an imprint of
Penguin Random House LLC, in 2021
First published in hardback in Great Britain by HarperCollins *Children's Books* in 2021

3 5 7 9 10 8 6 4 2

ISBN: 978-0-00-849619-7

HarperCollins *Children's Books* is a division of HarperCollins*Publishers* Ltd
1 London Bridge Street, London SE1 9GF

www.harpercollins.co.uk

HarperCollins*Publishers*
1st Floor, Watermarque Building, Ringsend Road, Dublin 4, Ireland

Text copyright © Drew Daywalt 2021
Illustrations copyright © Oliver Jeffers 2021

Published by arrangement with Philomel, an imprint of Penguin Random House LLC

Printed in Latvia

GREEN
is for
CHRISTMAS

ACTUALLY, RED is for CHRISTMAS, but please tell me more.

DREW DAYWALT
OLIVER JEFFERS

GREEN
IS FOR
CHRISTMAS

GREEN is For HOLLY

RED

IS FOR

CHRISTMAS

RED

IS FOR

candy

canes

Even
OLD
ones.

GREEN
is For
Fir
TREES

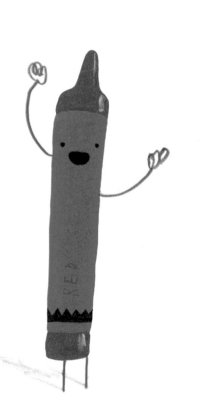

RED
IS FOR
SANTA
CLAUS

Listen, you guys.
I'm INVISible
ALL YEAR long.
so you're NOT
TAKing this one
Away From ME.

HELLO!

Snowflakes?
SNOW MEN?
MARSHMallows?

WHITE
is For
christmas

I'm kind of a **BIG DEAL** on the CHRISTMAS TREE.

HELLO!

SILVER
is For
CHRISTMAS

what about cookies
and REINDEER?

BROWN
IS FOR
CHRISTMAS

I'm more
Burnt Sienna,
but that's cool!

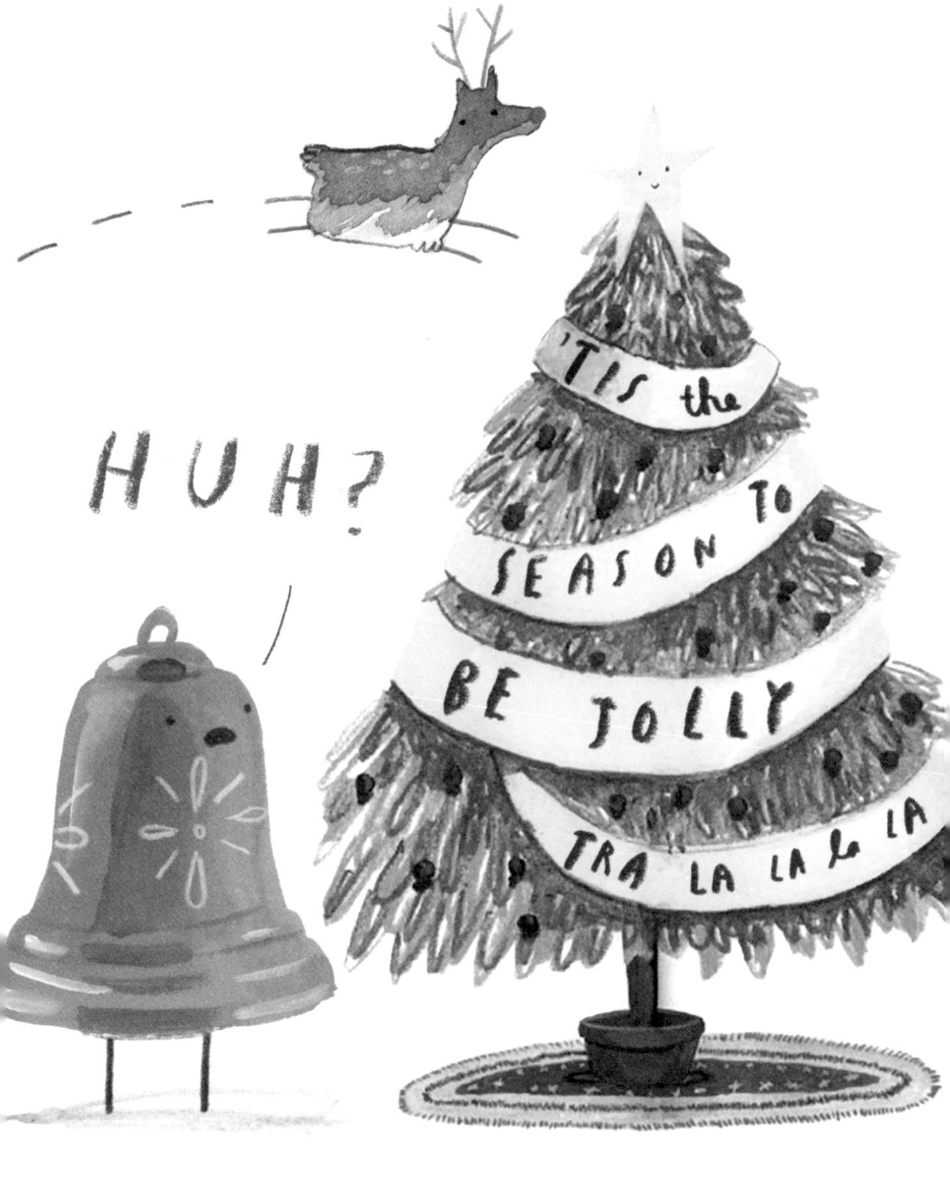
HUH?
'TIS the SEASON TO BE JOLLY TRA LA LA La LA

YOU CAN'T HAVE WITHOUT ANY

Especially
Green!